THE MANSIONS OF THE GODS

TEXT BY GOSCINNY

DRAWINGS BY UDERZO

TRANSLATED BY ANTHEA BELL AND DEREK HOCKRIDGE

HODDER DARGAUD
LONDON SYDNEY AUCKLAND

ASTERIX IN OTHER COUNTRIES

Australia	Hodder Dargaud, Rydalmere Business Park, 10/16 South Street, Rydalmere, N.S.W. 2116, Australia
Austria	Delta Verlag, Postfach 10 12 45, 7000 Stuttgart 1, Germany
Belgium	Dargaud Bénélux, 3 rue Kindermans, 1050 Brussels, Belgium
Brazil	Record Distribuidora, Rua Argentina 171, 20921 Rio de Janeiro, Brazil
Canada	(French) Dargaud Canada, Presse-Import, 307 Benjamin Hudon, St Laurent, Montreal, Quebec H4N 1J1, Canada
	(English) General Publishing Co. Ltd, 30 Lesmill Road, Don Mills, Ontario M38 2T6, Canada
Denmark	Serieforlaget A/S (Gutenberghus Group), Vognmagergade 11, 1148 Copenhagen K, Denmark
Finland	Sanoma Corporation, P.O. Box 107, 00381 Helsinki 38, Finland
France	Dargaud Editeur, 6 Rue Gager-Gabillot, 75015 Paris, France
	(titles up to and including Asterix in Belgium)
	Les Editions Albert René, 26 Avenue Victor Hugo, 75116 Paris, France
	(titles from Asterix and the Great Divide onwards)
Germany	Delta Verlag, Postfach 10 12 45, 7000 Stuttgart 1, Germany
Greece	Mamouth Comix Ltd, Ippokratous 57, 106080 Athens, Greece
Holland	Dargaud Bénélux, 3 rue Kindermans, 1050 Brussels, Belgium
	(Distribution) Betapress, Burg. Krollaan 14, 5126 PT, Jilze, Holland
Hong Kong	Hodder Dargaud, c/o Publishers Associates Ltd, 11th Floor, Taikoo Trading Estate, 28 Tong Cheong Street, Quarry Bay, Hong Kong
Hungary	Egmont Pannonia, Pannonhalmi ut. 14, 1118 Budapest, Hungary
Indonesia	Penerbit Sinar Harapan, J1. Dewi Sartika 136D, Jakarta Cawang, Indonesia
Italy	Mondadori, Via Belvedere, 37131 Verona, Italy
Latin America	Grijalbo-Dargaud S.A., Aragon 385, 08013 Barcelona, Spain
Luxemburg	Imprimerie St. Paul, rue Christophe Plantin 2, Luxemburg
New Zealand	Hodder Dargaud, P.O. Box 3858, Auckland 1, New Zealand
Norway	A/S Hjemmet (Gutenburghus Group), Kristian den 4des gt. 13, Oslo 1, Norway
Portugal	Meriberica-Liber, Avenida Duque d'Avila 69, R/C esq., 1000 Lisbon, Portugal
Roman Empire	(Latin) Delta Verlag, Postfach 10 12 45, 7000 Stuttgart 1, Germany
Southern Africa	Hodder Dargaud, c/o Struik Book Distributors (Pty) Ltd, Graph Avenue, Montague Gardens 7441, South Africa
Spain	Grijalbo-Dargaud S.A., Aragon 385, 08013 Barcelona, Spain
Sweden	Hemmets Journal (Gutenberghus Group), Fack, 200 22 Malmö, Sweden
Switzerland	Dargaud (Suisse) S.A., En Budron B, 1052 Le Mont sur Lausanne, Switzerland
Wales	(Welsh) Gwasg Y Dref Wen, 28 Church Road, Whitchurch, Cardiff, Wales
Yugoslavia	Nip Forum, Vojvode Misica 1-3, 2100 Novi Sad, Yugoslavia

JP
820810

The Mansions of the Gods

ISBN 0 340 17719 5 (cased)
ISBN 0 340 19269 0 (limp)

First published in Great Britain 1973 (cased)
This impression 92 93 94 95 96

First published in Great Britain 1975 (limp)
This impression 92 93 94 95 96

Published by Hodder Dargaud Ltd,
Mill Road, Dunton Green, Sevenoaks, Kent TN13 2YA

Printed in Belgium by Proost International Book Production

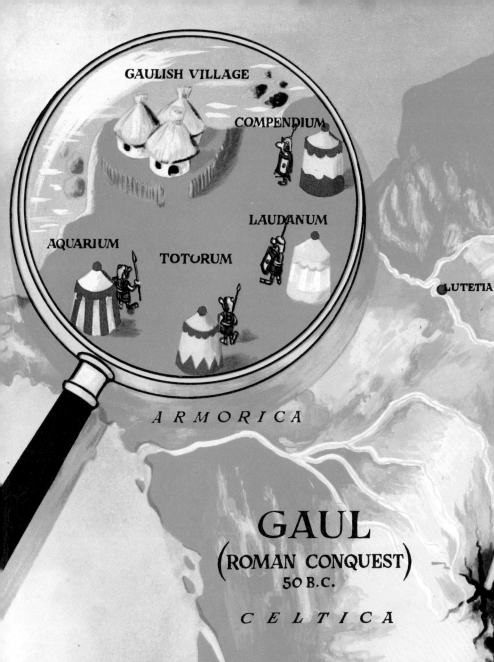

GAUL
(ROMAN CONQUEST)
50 B.C.

BELGICA

LUTETIA

ARMORICA

CELTICA

AQUITANIA

PROVINCIA

GAULISH VILLAGE

COMPENDIUM

LAUDANUM

AQUARIUM

TOTORUM

e year is 50 BC. Gaul is entirely occupied by the Romans.
ll, not entirely… One small village of indomitable Gauls still
ds out against the invaders. And life is not easy for the
man legionaries who garrison the fortified camps of
orum, Aquarium, Laudanum and Compendium…

7

THE BOARS ARE RATHER RETIRING TODAY!

THEY GO INTO HIDING WHEN THEY SEE A CROWD

THESE FORESTS AREN'T PROPERLY KEPT UP. WE OUGHT TO BE SNIFFING OUT ROMANS

WE'RE HERE TO SNIFF OUT BOARS, OBELIX

LOOK, ASTERIX! DOGMATIX IS COMING ON! THERE'S SOMETHING MOVING IN THAT THICKET!

LEAVE IT TO ME!

EEEEEK!

?!

CAN'T YOU LET ME GO ABOUT MY BUSINESS IN PEACE?

YOU HAVEN'T ANY BUSINESS HERE!

WHAT'S MORE, YOU'RE FRIGHTENING THE BOARS AWAY!

BIFF!

SOON AFTERWARDS...

WELL, IT'S QUITE TRUE! I DON'T LIKE PEOPLE TO FRIGHTEN THE BOARS! POOR THINGS, THEY'RE SCARED OF STRANGERS... WE'RE DIFFERENT; THEY'RE USED TO US

I'LL HAVE TO HAVE A WORD WITH OUR CHIEF. IT'S NOT NORMAL FOR ROMANS TO BRAVE THE DANGERS OF THE FOREST, ESPECIALLY WHEN THE DANGERS ARE US!

ROMANS IN THE FOREST ?!?

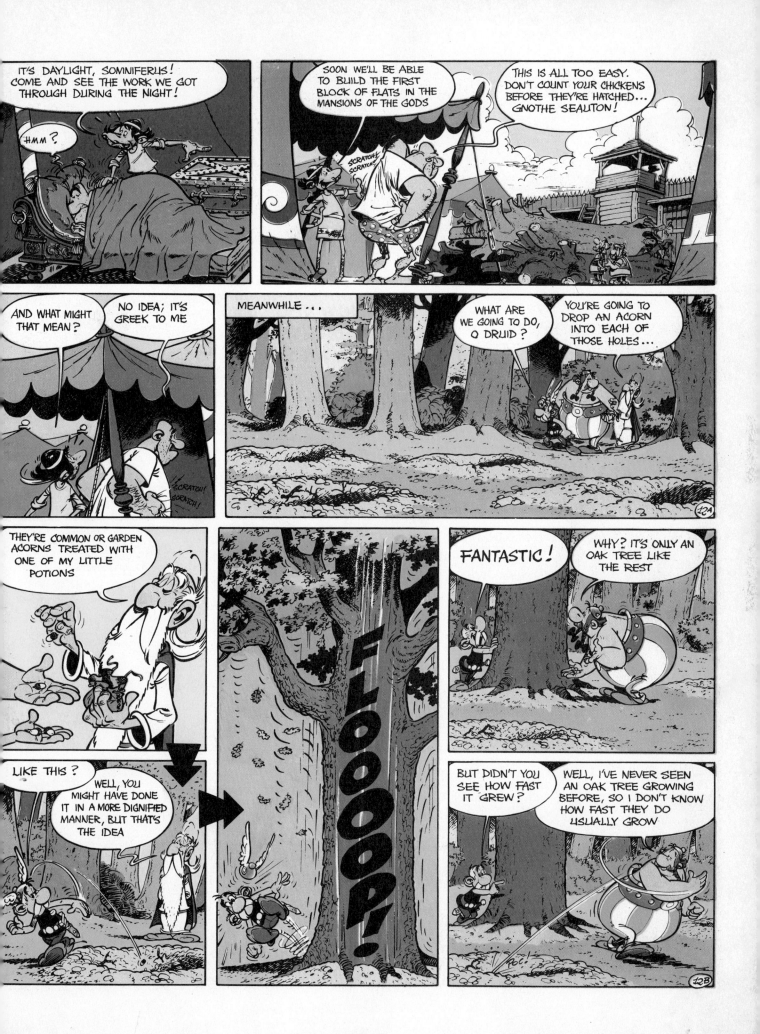

19

WOVLD YOV LIKE TO LIVE LIKE A GOD ? IF SO... THE MANSIONS

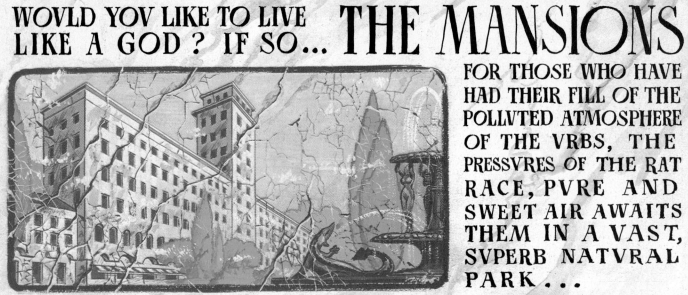

FOR THOSE WHO HAVE HAD THEIR FILL OF THE POLLVTED ATMOSPHERE OF THE VRBS, THE PRESSVRES OF THE RAT RACE, PVRE AND SWEET AIR AWAITS THEM IN A VAST, SVPERB NATVRAL PARK...

LESS THAN THREE WEEKS AWAY FROM THE CENTRE OF ROME AND JVST ONE WEEK FROM THE CENTRE OF LVTETIA (GAVL)

A HEALTHY AND HAPPY LIFE,

AT DAWN, WOKEN BY THE MELODIOVS SONG OF THE GAVLISH COCKEREL, THE ROMAN MATRONS GET VP, AS WELL AS THEIR HVSBANDS AND CHILDREN. WHILE THE HVSBAND IS VISITED BY THE BARBER (BOVGHT LOCALLY), THE LADY OF THE HOVSE ARRANGES FOR JENTACVLVM TO BE SERVED TO THE CHILDREN, WHO ARE GETTING READY FOR SCHOOL. ONLY THEN WILL SHE CALL HER HAIRDRESSER FOR HER MORNING SET, WHILE WATCHING THE WILD BOARS FROLIC ON THE LAWNS OF THE PARK...

IN THE SCHOOLS OF THE MANSIONS OF THE GODS, THE EDVCATION OF THE CHILDREN IS ENTRVSTED TO SPECIALLY SELECTED SLAVES, WHO REPORT ON THE PROGRESS OF THEIR PVPILS AT THE MEETINGS OF THE PARENT-SLAVE ASSOCIATION. THIS ARRANGEMENT ALLOWS FOR THE VSE OF THE WHIP EITHER ON THE PVPIL OR THE SLAVE, IF THERE ARE DIFFERENCES OF OPINION. WHILE THE CHILDREN ARE AT SCHOOL, THE HVSBAND GOES TO WORK. IF HE WORKS IN ROME, HE COMES HOME EVERY SIX WEEKS FOR A GOOD NIGHT'S REST.

OF THE GODS ARE FOR YOV!

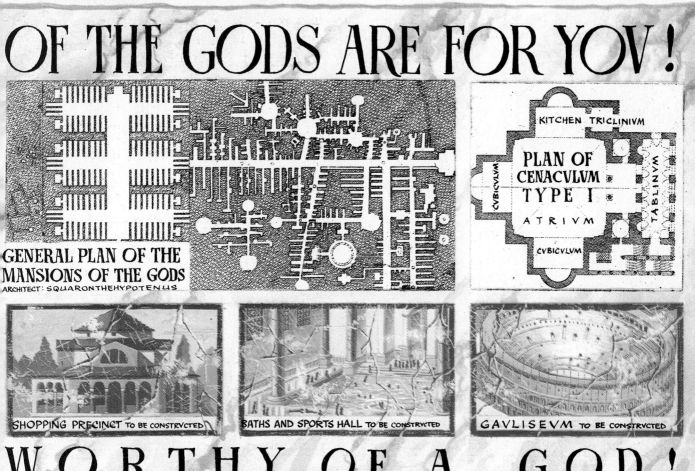

GENERAL PLAN OF THE
MANSIONS OF THE GODS
ARCHITECT: SQUARONTHEHYPOTENUS

PLAN OF
CENACVLVM
TYPE I
KITCHEN TRICLINIVM
CVBICVLVM
ATRIVM
TABLINVM
CVBICVLVM

SHOPPING PRECINCT TO BE CONSTRVCTED

BATHS AND SPORTS HALL TO BE CONSTRVCTED

GAVLISEVM TO BE CONSTRVCTED

WORTHY OF A GOD!

ONCE HER HVSBAND AND CHILDREN HAVE GONE, THE MATRON VISITS HER FRIENDS FOR XI SES. AFTERWARDS SHE MAY GO TO THE SHOPPING PRECINCT (TO BE CONSTRVCTED) WHERE SHE CAN FIND ALL SHE NEEDS, FROM FOOD AND CLOTHES TO JEWELLERY AND SLAVES. SHE IS HAVING A DINNER PARTY, AND SHE'S ONE SLAVE SHORT? SHE GOES STRAIGHT TO THE SELF-SERVICE SLAVE MARKET! SOON THE FAMILY WILL BE HOME. IT IS TIME TO PREPARE THE CENA.

WHEN THE HVSBAND COMES HOME FROM WORK HE CAN VISIT THE BATHS AND THE SPORTS HALL WITH HIS FRIENDS, OR GO FOR A ROMANTIC STROLL WITH HIS WIFE ALONG THE SHADY FOOTPATHS OF THE PARK (WHERE THE WILD BOARS FROLIC). IN THE EVENING, HE CAN GO TO THE GAVLISEVM (TO BE CONSTRVCTED), OR SIMPLY HAVE A FEW FRIENDS IN FOR AN ORGY. ALL HE HAS TO DO THEN IS GO TO BED AND AWAIT THE DAWNING OF A MAGNIFICENT NEW DAY, THE SORT OF DAY YOV CAN FIND ONLY IN THE MANSIONS OF THE GODS!

NEXT MORNING

GETAFIX, LOOK HOW OUR VILLAGE HAS CHANGED! AND THAT'S NOT ALL...

FISHMONGER

ANTIQUES

ANTIQUES

FISHMONGER

ANTIQUES

DEAR ME, NO...

...THE WONDERFUL SPIRIT OF CO-OPERATION WE USED TO HAVE HAS DISAPPEARED

NOW I'M CERTAIN, ASTERIX. ALL THIS IS PART OF JULIUS CAESAR'S PLAN TO GET RID OF US!

I'LL SELL MY FISH CHEAPER THAN YOURS!

CAN YOU SEE MY FISH? CAN YOU SEE IT?

WHO WANTS TO FEEL MY ANTIQUE?

CAESAR IS USING THE ROMANS WHO LIVE IN THE MANSIONS OF THE GODS, BUT THEY DON'T REALIZE WHAT IS HAPPENING

WE MUST GET RID OF THEM... I'VE GOT AN IDEA

NEXT MORNING

A VACANT FLAT IN THE MANSIONS? AFRAID NOT, EVERYTHING'S TAKEN – IT'S A GREAT SUCCESS!

SOON WE'RE GOING TO CUT DOWN THE REMAINDER OF THE FOREST AND BUILD SOME NEW FLATS. WE COULD RESERVE YOU ONE OF THOSE...

TEEHEE! IF THE GAULS ARE STARTING TO LEAVE THE VILLAGE, THE LAST CENTRE OF RESISTANCE AGAINST THE ROMAN OCCUPATION WILL HAVE DISAPPEARED. CAESAR WILL BE DELIGHTED!

THAT SAME AFTERNOON, IN THE VILLAGE...

ANTIQUE

FISHM

GRRRRRRRR!

AAAAH!

OBELIX! CALM DOWN, OBELIX, TAKE IT EASY!

GRRRRR

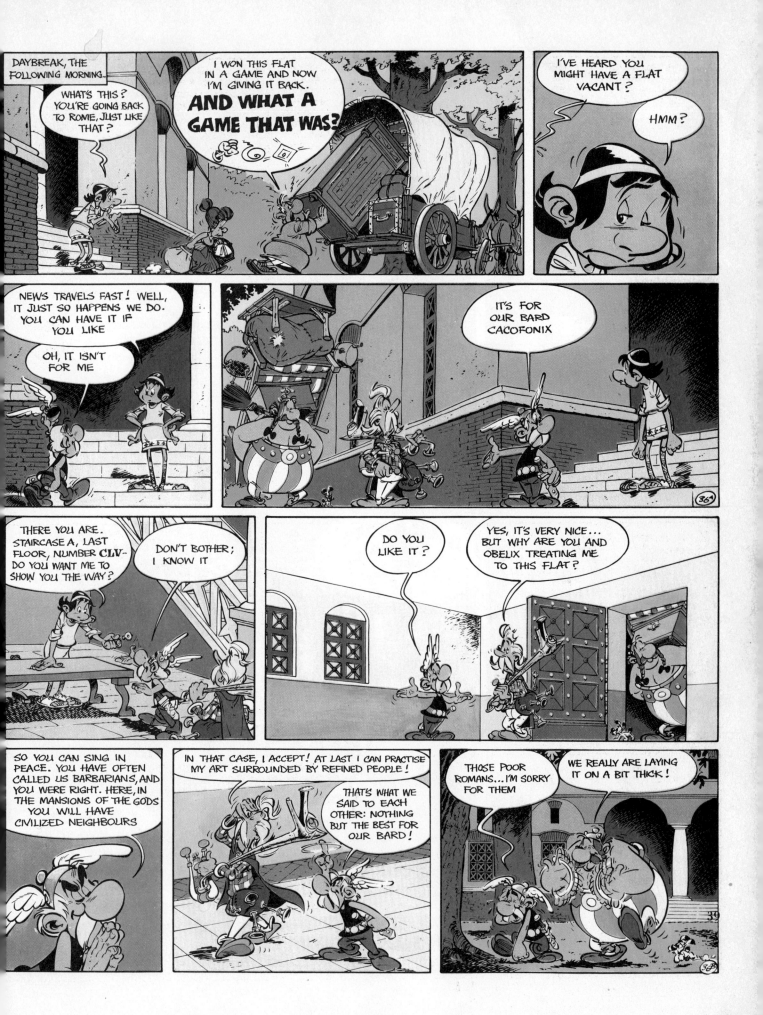

40

41

PRINTED IN BELGIUM BY
proost
INTERNATIONAL BOOK PRODUCTION